Caprice

Matthew Lotti

ISBN-10: 0-9715594-2-2
ISBN-13: 978-0-9715594-2-4

Library of Congress Control Number: 2002095594

Dedicated to the memory of Jim Thompson

"Victims suggest innocence. And innocence, by the inexorable logic that governs all relational terms, suggests guilt."

- Susan Sontag

one.

Two men were sitting in a room. One of them - the man to the right - was wearing a blue suit and had his hair slicked back like a gangster from the 30's. The other man, seated to the left, was wearing a blue suit but was starting to lose his hair - it was not exactly noticeable yet, but the temples were receding ever so slowly, glacier-speed - and he would, no doubt, look like his father and his grandfather and his own older brother that he never spoke of nor cared to see in the next couple of years.

The room was uncharacteristically packed with paper of all sorts: legal books, documents, trials, transcriptions, lost artifacts from the complaints and procedures of yesteryear, problems that had long since been solved and probably forgotten. There was barely enough room to sit and free one's elbows and relax and think and breathe.

The man with the (slightly) receding hair - Lucien - looked up from the paper he was diligently scribbling on to speak to Jacob - the other man with the blue suit - who was simultaneously jotting down ideas and plans on a yellow-lined piece of scrap paper before him. Lucien spoke:

"I was reading, the other day, the story of a woman. Just an ordinary woman, don't remember what she did for a living. One night, I think … yeah, I think it was July; she was outside playing catch with her daughter. Just running, playing, jumping - you know, enjoying herself, her time with her kid. As the sun was starting to set, and it was getting a little cooler out, she brought her daughter in, washed her up, put her to bed. She herself washed up, shampooed her hair, toweled herself off, and made herself a drink - sweetened iced tea, it was. She then sat back, clean, comfortable, turned on the TV, maybe a sitcom, maybe a film. A classic movie. It never said what, exactly. So she finished off her drink, set the glass aside, laid down and fell asleep. Come morning, woke up around, oh, 10-something and made her daughter some breakfast - she heard her in the other room, watching television. Her husband, well, he was on a business trip, several hundred miles away. She could be a single mom for all I remember. But that morning, she got up, stretched, put on her slippers, the light ones that don't make your feet sweat, and made her way over to the bathroom to brush her teeth and comb her hair, maybe floss. And she looked into the mirror, and as she gazed into the mirror, she saw her face, and it was covered in blood - her blood. It was running down her cheeks. It looked as if it was coming out of her eyes. She rubbed, and more trickled down. Small, thin streams, like tinted sweat. She looked at her neck. It had made its way down there. There was a little on her nightshirt. She started to panic. Oh my God. She rubbed more, and it got all over her fingers. She dashed out of the bathroom. The doorbell may have been ringing but she couldn't notice it or pay it mind. She called her doctor. He told her to go immediately to the hospital. She grabbed her daughter by her arm - her daughter, upon seeing her mother, was understandably frightened. She got there with some difficulty, not dialing 911 or anything like that, deciding to get there herself, and she was treated too. After some questioning and testing - the woman had to be put through countless tests and see countless men and women she did not know nor wished to know - there was this neurologist that tells her, in plain English, that what she had, in his professional opinion, was a brain tumor. The size of a golf ball. In her head. She just woke up, and there it was. It had formed over time, but that day, in July, it reached its limit."

Having heard all this, Jacob, naturally stunned, asked, "Did she die?" It seemed like the proper thing to ask following a tragic monologue of that length.

"I don't think so," Lucien said, "but that's not entirely the point."

"Then what is?"

"The point is that any second, a nightmare can occur."

Jacob shrugged. "But that sounds like a rare case, don't you think?"

"Do you like statistics?"

"They're a part of life."

Silence, for a moment, took over the conversation. Both men refocused and returned to their work.

"And in July...," Lucien murmured softly to himself, but the three words were still audible.

He received no reply.

two.

The next morning, Lucien was in bed with his wife of twelve years, Erika. They decided to marry as soon as Lucien got out of Dickinson, having gone through a plethora of coursework and prepared to set up shop, as it were. Erika had once, in her life, desired to become an attorney for whatever reason that moves people to do things with their lives, but had given up that desire once her more-than-capable better half entered the field. Her grandmother, a saintly woman with nothing but malice on her lips, had told her that two lawyers married together would bring nothing but bad luck to the family, although Erika always suspected her grandmother got that impression from watching *Adam's Rib*.

Before the alarm rang, Erika got out of bed, stood up, stretched slightly, stepped into her mauve slippers to the right of the bed (her side - it's always territorial) and walked to the front of the room, where she gazed at herself in the full-length mirror she purchased at Ethan Allen as an impulse-buy.

Lucien, noticing her absence, glanced at the digital clock out of crusty, half-dreamy eyes and managed to form words with what was a seemingly limited supply of air. "Why so early?"

"I'm going to have breakfast with Alissa. Remember?"

A pause. "Oh," and then a sigh, "but I thought it was always on Thursdays."

"They have this project they're doing over there, so she can't do it this Thursday."

"Could you skip this week?" Lucien sat up on his elbows and rolled his neck around.

"What?"

"Nothing."

Erika freed herself from the mirror's hold and walked towards the bathroom, entered, and shut the door softly behind her. The sound of the vent in the bathroom was loud. To compensate, Lucien had to raise his voice, which was, at that time of the day, a real strain.

"Why don't you two ever meet for lunch instead? Why always breakfast? And the three of us haven't gone out for dinner lately. You know I like Alissa."

No answer. He slid back down into the sheets, content to close his eyes again and not repeat himself.

———

Lucien got into work at 9 AM. The office he spent most of his time in was meticulously designed and maintained, unlike the other rooms of the building, which tended to be treated poorly and packed with useless junk their slovenly inhabitants were too lazy to dispose of, waiting for the cleaning crew to take it away. All his materials were color-coded and arranged alphabetically - with less of a focus on wall decorations (such as posters, paintings or photographs) and more on cautiously spaced out shelves and chairs. Two portraits done by a friend of a friend - one of John Grisham, one of Gregory Peck in *To Kill a Mockingbird* - both created with graphite and pastel on Rives paper are the only things resembling 'art' in the entire room, and both were situated directly across from Lucien's desk, so that their gazes met his every time he looked up.

On his desk, he had a laptop computer and was documenting his morning routine. He found this cathartic and soothing, like coffee. It read:

7:55: Spoke with wife re: her morning arrangements. Questioned why she was going to have breakfast with Alissa today instead of Thursday, which is when she always goes. Was informed that Alissa has plans set up for Thursday, thereby rearranging everyone *else's* plans. Asked to accompany the two of them sometime, out of kindness, but was received coldly.

8:15: Pulled myself out of bed, went to counter, and examined facial hair. Potential ingrown hair found under jaw, lower-left side. Used MintyFresh dental floss to clean upper row of teeth...

... but his documenting was interrupted by a knock on the door. It was Jacob, in a beige turtleneck. He walked in.

"I see Hilberto Jones is out in the hallway," he said.

"Yes, I know. Keep him sitting," Lucien answered.

Jacob took a quick peek outside and then shut the door completely. "There's a rumor going around town that - well, do you remember Delphine Whitney? The redhead who worked for...?"

"Yes, I remember."

"What did you think of her?"

"Well," Jacob said, sneaking closer to the desk, "Angie told me she's going after Carl in City Hall for sexual harassment."

"About time somebody did. You know *that* guy."

"Pete got Carl the other day. They talked for three hours."

"Who does Delphine have?"

"Don't know. She has documentation, from what I heard."

"He'll slide." A pause. "You know what? Bring in ... ummm...."

Jacob opened the door and stepped into the hallway. "He looks comfortable."

"Rattle him, then."

"All right." Jacob motioned to Hilberto to come back.

"Oh, wait, before you go I need a favor," Lucien said as he was placing his computer into its carrying case beside the desk. "After this meeting I'm going to be at the Court House for a bit, so can Courtney just handle all my calls, too?"

He thought for a moment, and then nodded. "She won't mind."

three.

The road to the Court House was long, long, winding and mostly uninteresting. Should one actually take note of such things, he or she would notice, during the drive:

> 9 churches
> 26 billboards advertising everything from fruit juice to Foodstuffs Supermarkets
> 1 pharmacy
> 18 stoplights
> 11 stop signs
> 4 run-down motels

... not to mention acres of farm land, dense forest packed with deer designed by God to (a.) run into your car and (b.) spread disease through ticks and the Frakes Bridge, which was about a half-mile long and crossed what may very well have been the River Styx, although, no doubt, the Styx was cleaner.

After the two-hour drive, and the proper turns, Lucien ended up sitting in the Court House parking lot, checking to see if all the paperwork and transcriptions were in his satchel. After verifying all was in order, he proceeded inside.

Lucien passed through the metal detectors with ease not simply because the objects on his person were non-metallic but the guard(s) that usually monitor(s) all incoming visitors was/were nowhere to be found. He easily navigated through the intricate hallway corridors, vacant as they were, using the pre-illustrated map already implanted in his brain.

Having flashed his Identification Card to a pygmy-like woman at a desk (filled out his name on a clipboard) and informed her of the name of the gentleman he was visiting, she picked up a phone, relayed the information to different people in other places inside the Court House, and then told Lucien he could proceed through. The detainee was being brought down.

The room that attorneys met with their clients, in this particular case, was approximately 15x15 feet in size, no windows, a square, wooden table with two chairs at either end, and the remains of a security camera dangling in the one corner. As he situated himself, a well-built man of about 35 named Stefan (with a slightly curved spine, causing him to lean forward a little) entered the room. The door Stefan entered from closed behind him. He seated himself in the chair opposite Lucien and was the first to speak.

"What's new, exactly?"

"Well," Lucien said, flipping through a thick, red-colored folder to find a stapled packet he swore he stored in there, "everything's going as it should. Smoothly. Which ... is good." A pause. "Erika sends her love."

"She hasn't visited me in two months and one week."

"I don't really know what's been going on with her. She's - she's just been in one of those moods lately. She'll work out of it."

Stefan shrugged dismissively. "It's no big deal."

Having found that packet of paper, Lucien set the folder down. "I have these, um, I think I have everything down on paper that we've spoken of and I've transcribed. For starters, well, I want to be painfully honest. I'm not going to...."

"You've said this before."

"I'm just reiterating what we know is true, or, actually, probable. It's not easy, you have to realize."

"And I appreciate it. I hope this hasn't sidetracked you at all."

Lucien exhaled, "For the two of us ... this has been a sore subject. I'm trying my best for you and for Erika, who does not feel good about having a blood relative in jail and is pushing for me to help you in any and every way possible. So, I kind-of concocted this 'plan,' and I'm going to try it." He leaned forward in his seat. "I'm going to drive to your hometown of Montgomery and just, you know, stay there, by your house in a cheap hotel for a couple of days. I just came up with this, it's still new, but if somehow I can just get talking to people there, someone has to be useful to us."

Stefan leaned back in his seat. "What good will that do? The police have pretty much done everything and talked to everybody."

"*I* want to talk to your boss, for one." He flipped over a page. "*I* want to talk to your neighbors, I want to talk to barflies, shop owners, everybody."

"It won't help."

"What else can I do? You, from ... well, you don't have many friends, I guess. No one you really spoke to regularly."

There was a long moment where one could almost see Stefan debating inside his mind as to whether or not to say something. Lucien, noticing this break, waited to speak.

"You could always meet with Isabella."

Dumbfounded, Lucien took a quick look at his documents. "Who is that again?"

"She was ... we were seeing each other off and on. On the side. Sometimes, not often."

"Wait, hold on. 'On the side?'" Another pause. "Who - you were having an affair? You, just wait a minute here.

You didn't bring this up before, did you? Because I don't *recall* you ever mentioning this...."

Interrupting, and speaking softer than normally to calm the excited Lucien, Stefan interjected: "I didn't want her involved in my problem."

"So you were sleeping together. Am I right?"

"I wouldn't call it an affair, exactly. It was...."

Lucien slammed his hand on the table. "No, you need to cut out this semantic shit. You need to be *explicitly clear* to me. I don't want *vagueness*. You have only got me left, do you understand? I want to know absolutely *everything*."

"All right, look -," he took the pen off the table, and a scrap of paper, and started writing, "- here's her ... last name ... address, phone number. Just - I don't want pressure on her. I didn't talk about her earlier because of what people would have thought. And no one knew about us. I'm sure of that."

"So 'the incident' was not instigated by her or done for her benefit?"

"Not at all."

"How can she help me, then?"

Stefan ran his hand across his shaved head. "She's a really sweet girl. I mean it. Darling."

"How can she help me?" Lucien repeated.

"Talk to her. She's intelligent. She'll come up with something."

"Does she have any more information than what you're giving me?"

"She's a very sympathetic person."

Lucien picked up his case and pulled out a different set of papers held together with a large paperclip that looked like a butterfly and started speaking with a newfound sense of patience, determined to get out of the room as soon as possible. "I've been reviewing the exact transcript of the day the events took place - you remember, the one we started together - according to you. And I really, really want to make sure everything on here is just ... it's just as close to perfect as you can be. I have decided to chart every fifteen minutes of the day from the moment you woke up to the moment you went to bed. I am giving this to you -" he slid the papers across the table, "- and here's the pen, and I want you to review the details in the time slots. I am going to sit here until you have written it all in there."

Stefan merely glanced at the packet. "You can't expect me to remember everything."

"I expect you to remember everything. We have -" he examined his watch, "- some time, but I have to leave soon. I want every pill swallowed, every glass of juice, every magazine article read, every block driven. Who did you see? Who did you talk to?"

Stefan picked up the pen and started filling in the minutiae stuffed into his memory and squeezed it into the margins (if need be).

"You said you had this 'raft' thing, correct?"

"Yes."

"And you mentioned that you built the raft by hand, didn't you? It's still in the woods right?" Lucien inquired.

"It should be. I don't see why not."

"Good. Write down directions on how to get to it. Also, one more thing - where's the best place to stay in Montgomery? A hotel? A motel?"

four.

Lucien did not like meatloaf in the least - he had sour memories of it from the boarding school cafeteria of his youth, and how the unwanted smell would work its way upstairs through hidden piping and holes in the building structure and rest comfortably in his and his roommate's bedroom, lingering for the duration of the day. Erika knew this from having been told about it multiple times, but consciously forgot, and therefore decided to make it for dinner, which did not please the master of the house when he encountered it at the end of his long day.

The two of them were seated at a rectangular table, not on opposite sides, but the same side, facing the miniature television set perched on the chair across from them (the stand it was on before was too ugly for them to bear and was removed). On TV: The Technology Network.

Erika got out of her chair to set her plate on the counter, and opened up the one cabinet to get a teabag out, for it was in the newspaper a week before that scientists started firmly and unwaveringly that green tea, when drunk after fatty meals, helped absorb some of the fat. People who drank tea tended to be healthier overall, harking back to the Chinese proverb: 'Better to deprive a man of food for three days than tea for one.'

Lucien was less interested in his plate than the TV, spending more time focusing on the talking heads and news blurbs than finishing his meal.

He spoke: "How was breakfast earlier?"

"It was good," Erika answered, "Crowded, but good."

"Where did you go? Collins'?"

"She picked the place - it's new. Opened last week. Umm... 'The Fruit Tree.'"

"Good?"

Silence.

"You saw my brother today."

"Yeah," Lucien said, standing to take his plate to the counter. "I really have to talk to you about that."

The microwave beeped. "Oh?"

"Well, it seems as if I need to drive and stay in Montgomery to look around for a few days."

Erika appeared confused. "Montgomery? Look around?"

"I really want to get a sense of the people there. I want to see the house. I want to get character information."

She took a sip: needed honey. "Isn't it too late for that? The trial is coming up."

"He's worried... and I need to go."

There was an uncomfortable silence. Erika's glare was fiery and intense, and while her eyes were fixed on her husband, her husband was doing his best to avoid looking back, sitting at the table, occupied by the television.

"It's a long drive, you know...." His voice trailed off.

Erika walked out of the room.

With his right hand in the shape of a paw, Lucien played around with the dinner knife left on the kitchen table, spinning it around.

five.

Lucien made sure he was up before his wife this time around - the earlier he left the quicker he'd have a chance to check into the hotel and start working. He also wanted proper time to reevaluate what he had packed for himself. He took a quick inventory for the vitals:

> clothing (five shirts, pants, ties, seven pairs of socks, seven pairs of boxers, etc.)
> medication (some needed, some not)
> cellular phone and charger
> one bottle of India ink
> one ream of printer paper
> two pens, two graphite pencils
> sketch pad
> laptop computer
> portable printer (lightweight, efficient)
> shaving supplies, shampoo
> (and then some)

He ate his Corn Pops cereal in peace, sans television, and had heated up a cup of English Breakfast tea. The car was loaded. Getting up, he went outside, locked the door and darted over to his BMW 720i. Just as he opened the door with his right hand, he realized that - to his left - was the ceramic cup of tea, with two swallows left in it. Not wanting to walk all the way back into the house and unlock the door and generate more noise, he set it right in the middle of the sidewalk.

———

Lucien did not have trouble finding Montgomery, which was situated approximately forty-five minutes away from the Court House, and because the directions were so detailed and accurate, and because the streets were devoid of traffic, and because the music in the car was so welcoming - the collected music of Matthew Shipp and his orchestra, the kind of sounds Erik Satie would have made had he not died when he was supposed to - it was an almost enjoyable drive.

The Record Hotel was not a fraction of the establishment Lucien was expecting to stay in for his business trip - it earned bonus points for the convenience of its location. All hotel rooms have traces of mankind in them, no matter how hard the hotel staff works or how expensive the hotel: semen stained bed sheets, traces of feces on the shower curtains, bacteria in the sink, urine and blood in the carpeting. The maids, being underpaid and mistreated and in a hurry, and not having to sleep in those rooms overnight, don't always get to everything. The Waldorf and the Best Western, microscopically, are both a mess.

Lucien spoke with the clerk at the front desk - a chinless chap in his mid-20's with spotty facial hair and a blank demeanor - about prices and the location of his room; Lucien was paying by credit card and fully intended on writing it off as a business expense.

After receiving the room key, he drove down a bit to his room (#206, the second floor of the two-tier hotel), unpacked his luggage and gear, and walked face-first into the familiar smell of bleach and detergent that is in all hotel/motel rooms. He had no need to really set up office at the moment - his main priority was to get out and examine his surroundings. While turning on and punching digits into his cell phone, he got out his sketchpad and his two graphite pencils. There was a woman who answered the phone - she was a secretary from the company Stefan worked for.

————

Since it was so pleasant outside, Lucien thought it would be a most delightful time to just wander around on foot, and take in the town, so he drove to Main Street, parked at a meter, and strolled up and down, venturing into the various bars, restaurants and coffee shops, ordering drinks or shots of espresso (a praline muffin at the one coffee shop), striking up conversations with random strangers, saying hello, how are you, that's fine, I'm glad, oh you don't say, well I'll be, you know why I'm here, what can you tell me, that's so interesting, let me write that down. Most people had precious little to offer aside from the things they knew and the things they overheard. The townspeople's collective unconscious was force-feeding Lucien the same story, and only minor details were altered or exaggerated, depending on the individual.

Lucien also took a drive out to Stefan and Gina's house - Gina being the deceased wife of Stefan - which was located smack dab in the middle of a giant grassy field, far larger in size than either deserved or earned by themselves. Gina's parents were taken care of by her grandparents (lumber, Canada) and the family was never without objects of luster. The house, dwarfed by the sheer size of the surrounding field, was still shiny and ivory, and gave off the impression of not being real - of being a toy mansion. Sitting on the gravel at the entrance gates, Lucien sketched what he saw with his #2 pencils on the sketchpad he made sure to bring with him. While drawing, he kept an eye on time, waiting for his pre-scheduled appointment.

six.

The office Stefan worked in was a part of a much larger, nondescript, monochromatic office building, shaped like a shoebox and just as aesthetically pleasing. Lucien ventured up to the third floor (of four total) on foot, finding the office with the greatest of ease and being welcomed by the receptionist, who he spoke with on the phone earlier. She said that Mr. Lacroix - Stefan's boss - was ready to see him and that he should just walk in. She pointed to a door to her right.

"So what exactly do you need from me?" Mr. Lacroix wanted to know, without a real formal introduction or greetings or how can I help you or smile or handshake, sitting in his ergonomic crimson office chair, surrounded by framed pictures of his daughter: his daughter at four months in the kitchen, his daughter in a carriage, his daughter with the family dog, no doubt named Sprocket, his daughter clinging to a tattered stuffed monkey, his daughter on her first day of kindergarten, his daughter covered in tempera during art "class" in the kitchen, etc. etc. All photos were either (a.) out of focus or (b.) poorly framed (the image was always de-centered).

"I want to know random things," Lucien said, paper and pen ready for use, "Impressions, stories, your opinions, mostly. As his superior."

"To be quite honest, what really sets me back is how he's not here now."

"I see."

"He tended to take up a great deal of work and get through it all in a hurry. He was real speedy. Christ, he made the rest of us look bad."

"Would you say...?"

"As a matter of fact," Mr. Lacroix continued, "he never took a lunch break. Never. He would ... run to the bathroom, run back. Usually had a sandwich in one hand, a pen in the other, and just kept on. Now we're all struggling to compensate, because he set expectations real high." Daughter in the Christmas Pageant dressed like an angel, daughter receiving her First Holy Communion....

"So," Lucien said, hastily noting all this down in longhand, "he was diligent. You would say that."

"Certainly."

"Mind if I, now, I don't know if you'd be willing to discuss how people got along with him or anything like that."

"None of us, well, hmmm ... we tried to leave him alone a lot. Didn't bother him. We knew he was there ... hell, we couldn't prevent his being there. But we didn't bother him or vice versa. No, no."

"Was he ever late?"

"No."

"Can you think of anything else, I don't know ... what did his position entail? Did he have a title?"

"He did whatever I told him to do."

"That does not help me in the least."

Mr. Lacroix looked stern and leaned forward. "Can I ask you a personal question?"

"You may."

"How many clients do you have?"

"Let me think...."

"Round figures. Approximations."

Lucien started mentally going through his files. Curiously, this number was never previously tallied, and yet it seemed so very important. He was shocked at himself for not thinking of it earlier. "I'm not positive, but just a rough number would be - actually, a lot of them are inactive, so, maybe ... forty? That's the number I'm coming up with. Not all forty in the same day, it's - it's hard to really tally such a thing." Daughter on a Ski-Doo, daughter playing soccer (wearing lucky #8), daughter in the National Honor Society group photo....

"No, that's fine, that's fine."

"I'm a public defender. That keeps me plenty busy."

Mr. Lacroix was looking at the pocket calendar on his desk.

"Sir, would you mind if I interviewed the staff here? Just to get their take on it?"

"Frankly," he responded, "I'd rather you didn't. We had a meeting about Stefan a while back and we basically felt that the incident shouldn't really be brought up again, for the mental health and working stability of the office and the office harmony that currently exists. We agreed that I would act as spokesperson for the office since we are all of the same opinion."

Lucien did little to disguise his disgust. "The reason I asked is because they may have more to offer me regarding him in stories, anecdotes and personal impressions. I'm trying to help Stefan out."

"I worked with him more than they did. I know him better."

"I'm guessing you have heard all the details of the case, then." Daughter at the prom with a well-groomed young man, daughter in front of her dorm at Cornell....

"What I read in the paper. It's sad to think about."

"Did you see it coming?" Lucien asked.

"Certainly not."

seven.

At their home, in the kitchen, standing in front of the refrigerator, Erika was using her cell phone to dial the number written on the paper napkin in her right hand.

This was her end of the conversation:

"Hi, Harold! How are you? Guess what? Yup. He's away. He's at ... some hotel. [Pause] Montgomery. Yeah. So is tonight okay? What? She is? Tell her I was thinking about her. Hmmm? Earlier. Yeah. Yeah. [Thinks] No. Well, do you want to meet here? Okay, that's fine. Wait. I'll get a pen."

She opened up the kitchen drawer and took out a blue pen and flipped over the paper napkin.

"Shoot. I love broiled - yeah. Right, right. Your turn this time. Ha! I'll see you there, then. Great, bye."

With the last 'bye,' she laughed loudly and turned off the phone.

———

In his room, Lucien was lying on top of the unruffled bed, face down, completely naked. He dialed the number on the white piece of paper, the number of the woman Stefan told him about.

This was his end of the conversation:

"Hello, is this ... um ... Isabella? Hi. You don't know me, but my name is Lucien Dargelos and I'm an attorney. [Pause] No, no, you're not in trouble, no, no you're not being sued. You know, I realize this sounds awkward, but I need to talk to you about a man you once knew. Wait - please don't hang up. Yes it is him, and he was the one who gave me your number. He thinks you can help me. [Pause] Technically, the two of us are related. Mm-hmm. He's my wife's brother. And, well, I spoke to him the other day. No, that's ... that's a police officer. I'm not a cop. [Laughs] Nothing like that. We ... can discuss that. [Pause] And that too. Your involvement, should you be willing to meet with me and talk with me, would be more than minimal. You don't have to, but ... oh. That's fantastic. I'm right ... you got it. I'm staying at a hotel. A hotel. [Pause] Oh, *the* hotel! Yeah. Are you comfortable with that, then? That's good. Tell me where it is...."

He wrote down the information on the paper in front of him.

"I'll see you at this place. What time? Okay. See you then."

After hanging up the phone Lucien got up, took two pills from two of the orange, translucent pill containers on the dresser - for his amusement, he stripped them of their labels - and went to shower.

eight.

The Marienbad Restaurant, a relatively new place with a somewhat pricey menu but with an extensive listing of cocktails and dessert, just had a mention in the newspaper, so that was the place Erika and her occasional Nighttime Companion #1, Harold, went to. It was Harold's idea to go there, and not having a better alternate, she agreed.

The two of them were seated at the table in the center of the dining area. In front of each was a pre-meal sake martini. It was their second of the night. Their dinner napkins - paper, oddly enough - were shredded and some pieces had found their way to the floor.

"It seems so...," Harold said.

Erika laughed. "Yes it does."

"Because we had only been talking...."

"Yeah." She was beaming.

"Briefly, though."

"Right." A pause. "They couldn't take their eyes off each other."

"Actually," he said, "that wasn't *the* worst incident."

Erika began laughing again, "You're *kidding*."

"No, the worst one ... I, she was so ... feisty and independent. And she just didn't need me. We were together a year and a half."

"Oh."

"Yes, and I know, that was a bit. But we were together *that* long, and I was trying to get out of my folks' house. Desperately. You know how it is."

She adjusted her skirt and smoothed out the fabric. "Entirely too well. Wait - how old were you then? 22?"

"Twenty-two," he grinned, shook his head, "and I didn't do anything my parents wanted me to at that time. I was so damn stubborn. I told you all about that, didn't I? The last time we met?" He paused. "Do you remember? For the life of me, I can't remember when it was. Was it something like, uh, 5 or 6 months ago? That's a long time. I really enjoy seeing you."

"He's always around," she responded.

"And now he's not. I understand. Anyway, here's the story of my worst incident. I'm working at an all-night diner. Not really into waking up early. Still not. Anyway, my ex, she's a regular at this dismal little place. She shows up with this crowd one night, that crowd another night, this guy, that guy - I have no idea who the hell they all are. They just sit there and talk and order one thing and one thing only - a bowl of cereal or a muffin or a cup of regular coffee, and they sit for hours and talk and light up endlessly, in a chain. One night she comes in alone ... this girl, Sarah is her name ... did I mention that?"

"No."

"She's sitting there, alone. For once, she's not surrounded by her friends or sisters or budding rock stars, it's just her. And I'm ... just interested in her. I'm -," he whispers, "- turned on by her *ease*. She's not a tramp, she dresses well, and just seems so at home, so confident. I remember her hair, the color was like burnt sienna. And she, now I normally hate piercings of any kind, but she has a hoop through her eyebrow, and I'd normally look at something like that and just ... hate it, but on her, it looked *cute*. She exuded that: cuteness. Cuteness and confidence." He laughed. "So when I approach her, alone, sitting, looking out the window into the darkness, I approach her, make this glib remark. I say: 'I've noticed you've been in here a lot. Since it isn't the ambience it must be to see me.' Hey, it's the only thing I could come up with. But it worked, and I guess she thought I was charming, or goofy."

"It's hard coming up with witty opening lines. At least it wasn't crass," Erika said.

"It was innocent, yes, certainly. Well, that night, I made her a hamburger on two seedless buns and with two pickles and no onions and exactly eighteen french fries. I -," he chuckled, "- am amazed I remember that, and she eats, and sits, waiting for me. I never asked why she waited or where her friends were, though later on I found out."

"Where?"

"They ditched her and went to Montreal. To shop, I guess. Maybe ride the power boats, walk around."

"I see."

"So with her, we went out to the usual spots around town on the weekends, and eventually she wanted to get this small apartment for the two of us."

Erika smiled. "It all leads to that."

"It's cozy, you know, it's cramped, cheap, old carpets, but to me, it's the greatest thing. I'm with her, it's, it's just right. But there's a lot in-between, and I don't want to delve into too much, but anyway, one day, she just, gets sick of me for whatever reason. I'm still not sure why."

"Did you do anything to hurt her?"

Harold stopped and thought for a moment, going through all the incidents he judged as being the catalyst, but couldn't come up with anything he thought was significant. "Maybe the little things. Your usual combination of quirks."

"And she left?"

"I wished she had just left. But, she actually got this other guy - I don't know where she met him - to come after me one night and beat me up ... badly. I was coming out of work...."

"You were leaving?" she asked, shocked.

"My shift was over, and this guy was just there. He pulls me down, and just wails and wails and wails with, I'm thinking it's like a pipe, or...."

"Oh my God."

"I'm just grateful it wasn't worse. I don't know what the weapon was. All I know is that I was in the hospital for a few weeks. The ambulance came and took me there after my manager found me."

"How did you know this guy or whomever was sent by her?"

"Well, I'm not done. It's not over. I tried to press charges, but this person fled, and no one saw this guy at all. No one. When I returned to the apartment all her clothes were gone, and the place itself was vandalized, messes all over the floors, the walls smeared with food, my television was destroyed, my CDs were broken, the refrigerator was pushed over. It smelled unbearable. Guess who had to pay for it all."

Erika kept shaking her head. "I can't believe it."

"The apartment was in my name. She had no family in town. They knew she was in there with me, but she just disappeared. And I had to move back with my parents. And permanent liver damage. To top it off, the bill. That's the three."

"Plus, you lost the girl," she added.

"That was the worst experience of my life," he concluded.

"My worst experience doesn't come close to that, but it took me a long time to recover from. Did I ever tell you about it?" Erika asked. "I don't recall."

———

That same evening, Lucien met with Isabella in the parking lot of the Blue Danube, a local bar/restaurant she haunted and that she said would be a good place to talk over drinks. They shook hands in the lot after all the introductions and hellos and smiling. Lucien was quietly marveled by the petite Isabella's appearance - crimson sweater, pixie hair, light pink lipstick, skirt of appropriate length. After the in-person greetings, he opened the door and let her in first.

They took seats at the bar. Lucien swiveled around to look around. It was still early, so the place was not crowded, and there were multiple vacant tables cleared off. "Do you want to sit someplace besides here? Did you eat anything?" he asked.

She shook her head, not bothering to turn around. "I'm fine, thanks. Did you eat?"

"Yes," he lied. "You didn't have to get dressed up for this, you know. This isn't a meeting and it's in the most strictest confidentiality."

"Since so few people know, knew ... it's not like there's been any backlash or questioning. I sort-of battled with the idea, privately, that as the third party in this bizarre love triangle I'm partially responsible, but ... his wife, she was a sweet woman, and I never suggested he do ... anything like what he did."

Lucien heard none of this because he couldn't stop going over in his head the meeting with Mr. Lacroix. "Damn," he said aloud.

"What is it?"

"I forgot to ask Stefan's boss about how he thought Stefan got along with his wife - if he suspected marital problems."

Isabella scoffed. "He wouldn't know or care. No one did."

"Why?"

"Why should he care?"

"I spoke to him today. Elusive. You had to have suspected marital problems, didn't you?"

"They kept their troubles hidden. He rarely mentioned her. They seemed to function well. Well enough. They collected junk together. Went to garage sales, stocked everything in their garages. Most of it was worthless, but it was a hobby."

The bartender came in from a back room and apologized for keeping them waiting.

Isabella ordered first. "I'll have a gin and tonic."

"Make it two," Lucien said.

"What kind of gin?" the bartender asked.

"Bombay's good."

"Same," Lucien answered, and the bartender went to the end of the bar. He turned to her. "I went to the house today."

"Did you go inside?"

"You can't. But I needed to see it."

"We never quite went over why Stefan mentioned me to you, though. I can't help him. If you think about it, I can only hurt his case. The whole thing makes me nervous."

"You can't be too nervous or else you wouldn't have agreed to meet me," Lucien rationalized.

Isabella just looked at him, silent. The bartender brought the drinks.

"He's panicking," Lucien continued. "He's trying anything that will help. It's not like he's trying to blame anybody or make you look bad. He realizes what jail is like."

"Will I have to talk to anyone else besides you? Do I have to go and testify?"

Lucien put his hand on his chest. "I swear you will not have to go to court. I guarantee it. I just want a Personal History of you, how you two met, things of that nature. Exact details. I'll write them down. I want you to check them for accuracy."

She agreed, and sipped her drink.

nine.

The clock on the dresser in Erika and Lucien's bedroom read 1:06 AM. Both her and Harold were on the floor, undressed and twisted together. Their clothing was scattered throughout the room.

Harold gently massaged Erika's left thigh, behind her knee, slid his hand down her calf and began playing with her toes.

"Buñuel had a foot fetish," he said.

Erika closed her eyes. "Am I your Catherine Deneuve?"

"You're my little gum drop."

Both giggled.

———

Both Isabella and Lucien had found their way back to Lucien's hotel room, where they spent the night together. Lucien stirred first, but he was face down on the floor with only his pair of Calvin Klein boxers on and no t-shirt. He got up and noticed Isabella under the covers, purring softly.

A tad cold, he picked up Isabella's sweater and put it on, but could not locate his pants in the dark. He also could not see where his watch had landed.

He went looking for his car keys, and those were easy to locate: on the dresser, by the lamp. He took them and dashed outside to his car, which he remembered driving, unsteadily, just a few hours before. He opened the door, popped the hood, leaned in close to find the distributor cap and rotor, yanked them out, ran to the nearest garbage can - next to the light post that helped him see - and threw everything away. Running back, he closed the car door, and the hood, and went back into his room. He shut the door, set the keys back down, and resumed his position face down on the floor.

ten.

Isabella, waking before Lucien, spotted him on the floor and kicked him gently.

"I don't remember *that*." Her foot was pushing around the crimson sweater he was still wearing.

Lucien, slow to wake, muttered almost inaudibly, "How did we get here?"

"You drove."

"I did?"

"You insisted."

He turned over to face her and the light screaming in from the window. "Sleeping on the floor is supposed to be magnificent for your back."

"You're not that old. Can I have my sweater, please? I need it so I'm not walking outside in my bra."

"No shower?"

"Already took it," she said.

"Ah."

Lucien sat up, worked his way out of the sweater (it was a very tight fit) and handed it back. He got up, found the rest of his clothes (now that he was assisted by the sunshine), neglected to shower and hurried out with Isabella.

Outside, next to the BMW, he asked if she was running late.

She checked her watch. "Not yet."

"Did you ever notice how alcohol could sometimes lead to sexual intercourse?"

"Not really."

They both got into the car, and Lucien tried to start it up. Nothing. Again. Nothing. Again. Isabella looked concerned.

Lucien slammed his hand on the wheel. "Come on...."

She glanced at the dashboard. "Is there gas in there?"

"Gas has little to do with the car starting."

"And my car's still at the bar," she said.

Not giving up, he kept trying and trying. She opened her door and got out. "No one's around to jump us," she said, noticing his was the only car in the lot. "Where's your cell phone? Give me the keys to the room. I can make a call."

"Here," he said, angered. "I'll come in too. I need to get it towed."

The two reentered the room, where she called a friend of hers to pick her up and take her to her car. "She'll show up soon," she told him. He took out the phone book and looked for the number of a garage, settling upon "Pat's," because Patrick was a boyhood friend and malevolent fuck.

Fifteen minutes passed until her efficient friend - another 30-something brunette, like her - arrived and carried her off. Lucien repeatedly apologized for the inconvenience, but Isabella understood. Thirty-five minutes passed until somebody from Pat's - Pat himself? - came and just hauled the vehicle away, not asking any questions, not asking what happened, not attempting to operate the vehicle in the parking lot.

eleven.

Lucien was on the cell phone. He dialed the number, waited for about forty-five seconds, and then began speaking. He said:

"I hate to leave this on voice mail, honey, but the car's not working and I'll be here a few days until it's fixed. I have a bunch of typing to do so you don't have to come and get me. I hope all is full of love."

... then he pushed a button and hung up.

Behind on his work and truly eager to catch up, he turned on his laptop and attached the cable to the Epson printer he brought with him. He commenced typing out the precise details of his previous day and the morning of the day he was currently experiencing. He continued using his 'standard' fifteen-minute increments, really struggling with his memory to go over what he had done the day before. He found extreme difficulty with precise details, therefore he compensated by keeping his descriptions to a minimum:

7:00: Alarm went off. Got out of bed. Went to the bathroom to....

———

After completing the task of going through that self-developed documenting process, and reviewing notes he had kept on a variety of papers - he had compiled and organized them into a cohesive, singular piece - he took out his sketch pad and pencils and started walking. It was approximately 11:30 in the morning and he was in the mood to explore both the secluded areas of town and the popular areas. It was a part of his Process.

While walking along the creek that ran for some five or six miles away from the hotel - Lucien was a fast walker because of his long strides and cardiovascular training - he came across a bi-level, surrounded by an immaculate array of flowers, trimmed bushes, yard islands landscaped with craft and care and an ancient wheelbarrow resurrected from a garage sale and refurbished with chrysanthemums and tulips inside and, on the one side, a hand-painted picture of an old early-American cottage. A woman was on the side of the house, raking the leaves, and she took notice of Lucien pacing around.

"Hello," he greeted her.

She waved to him. "Hiya there."

"Do you need a hand with that?"

"No, I enjoy it."

Lucien walked closer to her. "I don't mind, really."

"So ... what do you think? Gardening and lawn care is my hobby. Being outside is my hobby."

"It's ... well-decorated. Pretty."

The woman pointed to his sketchpad. "Are you an artist?"

"I'm here on behalf of a former resident, Mr. Dargelos. I'm sure you know who that is."

"Yes. So tedious, don't you think?"

"Excuse me?"

"The news. Do you find things like that interesting? Everyday you hear something or read something, and it echoes what you've read about the day before or seen the day before. In a strange way, it's almost as if the same people are being killed."

Lucien wasn't sure how to respond. "Can I have a glass of water or something like that? I'm kinda thirsty."

"I'll have a glass of something myself," she said as she set down the rake and walked toward the front door.

"Need any help?" he volunteered.

"No, no, stay there."

Eventually, the woman came out of the house with two tall glasses. Lucien had taken a seat on a pile of the collected leaves and was sketching the wheelbarrow and flowers. She handed him his and accompanied him by sitting on the ground close by.

He took a gulp and almost choked. "What is this?"

"It's Yuengling. My grandson and his fiancée visited last week and he bought a case and never drank it all. It's taking up room in the refrigerator and I'm trying to get rid of it."

"Water would have been better," he said.

"My son is a lawyer. Practices in Oregon, of all places."

"One of my professors was from Oregon. I despised her immensely."

There was a break in the conversation and both seemed to drift off for a brief second. Lucien restarted the conversation by asking how his business was doing.

"He's getting by."

"It's all we can do," he mused.

Another pause. He swirled around the liquid in the cup.

"He's guilty as hell," she said. "You know that."

"Your son?" He tried not to smile.

The woman ignored that comment. "Stefan and his wife never got along. Always at each other. He would harass other people in public just to get under her skin. I've seen him do it in restaurants. That man had to be the goddamn center of attention."

"He always struck me as being low-key. People have given me completely different takes on him. I spoke to several folks yesterday around town. One couple said Stefan and his wife always got along well."

"Who said that?" she asked.

"They were relatives."

"What else did they say?"

"They said Stefan and his wife hid their extreme unhappiness."

She set her drink on the grass. "To be honest, I never did like him, even before."

"Why?"

"I've known him for a while. Just struck me as being abrasive. You know how there are some Hollywood stars you like, while others seem scummy and rub you the wrong way every time you see them? You hear people say, 'Oh, I don't like so-and-so, but I love so-and-so' based merely on appearance? Well, I think this might be the case with me, to look at it from both sides. You can't like everybody."

"So he was never hostile to you?"

"Not hostile. That's not the word. Never hostile. He was different. It's as simple as that. Just, he never ... I don't know. They were something like outsiders."

"He was eccentric, you mean?"

She nodded, "Did you hear about the raft?"

Lucien thought back to the brief conversation he had with Stefan over this raft. "He talked about it and I noted it down but I honestly thought nothing of it. They went down the river by here on the raft the Saturday of the incident."

"Did he tell you he made the raft by hand?" she asked.

"Sort-of."

"Built it. Didn't buy it, though heaven knows they could afford it. In fact, it's there, up the river on the embankment, right by a parking lot. After he and his wife went down the river he put it on a truck and drove it back to the starting point."

"And how do you know this?"

She coughed. "Friends and I go hiking up there sometimes, and we saw it. We purposely looked for it and we found it."

Pause.

"Honestly," Lucien said, "I think the idea of going on a homemade raft is interesting, don't you think?"

"If that's your thing," she said, nonchalantly.

"Is it still intact?"

"That I don't know. I wouldn't touch it."

Lucien got up, flung the remaining beer out of the glass and wiped off the leaves that were sticking to his clothes. "I should continue on, then. Before I go, could you write down what you just told me on this paper? About the raft? I need to find it." He handed her the sketchpad and one of his pencils. "This is all I have to write with." He already had a set of directions from Stefan, but wanted hers along with his.

"I'm not very good with directions," she admitted.

"Try," he said. He took a sweeping glance across the spacious yard. She printed the directions as carefully as possible. "You know, my wife and I always wanted to re-do our yard but never had time."

"Everyone should cultivate his or her garden," she mused, and smiled knowingly.

twelve.

Being car-less, Lucien had to find a source of transportation. The woman told him walking to the raft site would not be advisable, and that he should drive there instead. He attempted to call Isabella, but she never answered. It was then that he thought to ask the clerk who worked in the hotel office, because he definitely had a car.

"But I can't leave here," the clerk told him. "Who will look after the office?"

"It's a really big, important favor. Who is going to come by here? I'm the only guest. If anyone asks what was going on, I'll vouch for you."

The clerk chauffeured Lucien to the site specified on the paper in his own Ford Escort. He had a tough time convincing the clerk to take him, but his offer to pay for a full tank of gas and the clerk's having seen the *Days of Our Lives* episode presently showing on the TV caused him to change his mind.

The good directions combined with the fact that the clerk was born and raised in Montgomery got Lucien to the almost-hidden parking lot easily. Lucien got out of the car and started prowling around - the clerk, curious as to what was being sought after but not wanting to get in the man's way kept a healthy distance behind.

It took some time, but Lucien finally found the homemade raft, resting on the ground about two feet from the river, covered in leaves, branches and debris. Lucien handpicked the rubbish off the raft.

The size of the raft was about 6 feet by 6 feet, constructed of heavy planks of wood held together miraculously by rope, nails and God-knows what else. The decrepit monstrosity startled him, it being at once primitive and foreign, like something cavemen would have devised to find their way down river. How did he get it back to the launch point? Lucien wondered. Did he lift it alone? He couldn't have.

Both men were standing there, speechless. Lucien broke the silence. "Do you think it can float?"

"How the fuck should I know?"

"Wanna toss it in and see?" Lucien laughed.

"It isn't yours."

"Who's going to need it?" Pause. "I'll just leave it here for now, I guess. Let's get out of here."

thirteen.

Inside her private office, littered with shelves of books she had no intention of ever cracking or even giving the common courtesy of blowing the dust off, Erika picked up her phone, and decided to check her messages. After hearing Lucien's long-since recorded declaration she calmly listened to the robotic voice give her a list of options, and chose 'one' to delete it. She placed the phone on the receiver, stopped, thought, picked the phone back up, and dialed a new number from memory.

The person on the other line picked up on the third ring. Erika said: "Hello, it's Erika. How have you been? I know, I know, yes you haven't heard from me in a long time. I always get that. I guess it's because I'm so busy." The phone call was to Heath, who was Nighttime Companion #2 (mostly when Nighttime Companion #1, Harold, was unavailable).

———

Lucien had spent a good deal of time in front of his high-powered laptop, stomach down on his bed and typing frantically. The one wall of his hotel room was covered with the taped-up drawings he had been making along the way, and he would glance at them from time to time to regain perspective.

On the monitor the word "Reconstruction" appeared at the very top of the document, as its title, centered and with a size 20 font. Following that, on the next line, in size 14 font, were the words, "A Reenactment." Aligned left, several spaces down, was "Plans:," followed by copied-and-pasted text from Stefan's transcript/testimonial regarding the day of the incident. Slight alterations had to be made, naturally.

fourteen.

Erika and her date, Heath, met together at Alan's Bowling Alley at 7:00 after work. Erika appeared disinterested but not completely bored.

After rolling his first gutter ball, Heath walked over and sat across from her. "I hate to come here, but I couldn't think of any where else to go," he apologized.

"No, hey, I haven't done this since I was 16, so it's certainly a change of pace. We could go to the movies afterwards, if you want." She examined her watch. "It's still early."

"I checked the listings," he said. "Not much looks interesting."

"It's too bad there isn't a beach within driving distance."

"We could always go hiking," he offered.

"At night?"

He laughed. "Hey, I'm just brainstorming. We could probably just get dinner and a drink."

"The dilemma we have here, I believe, is universal," she began. "Think of it: everywhere the world over, people are asking each other what to do. And they're struggling with the lack of choices. Small towns, big cities - in the latter, there are too many options, and you just wind up paralyzed by the fear of making a poor decision. In the former, there aren't any options at all. It's the story of our weekends: constant stagnation."

"That's interesting," he said while scratching the back of his unnaturally long neck, "but I'm not sure I completely agree."

———

In Lucien's hotel room, there were plates of food spread out on the bed and some were lined up on the dresser in the front of the room. There was a knock on the door.

"Come in," he yelled, and in stepped Isabella.

"Smells like a bistro in here," she said.

"I hope this is all right. The restaurant delivered, and I ordered a little of everything."

fifteen.

At the Gemini, a respected eatery on the west side of town, Erika had met up with Heath for dinner. One of the establishment's 'novelties' was a table covering made of paper and a cup of Crayola crayons for patrons to doodle with (it was not simply for children, either, for adults found it to be a delightful quirk). The Gemini specialized in quiches, but neither ordered the quiche special.

Erika was using the crayons to color her cloth napkin - not the table - which piqued Heath's curiosity. "What is that?" he asked, examining the non-descript design. He didn't want to question why she wasn't using the paper table covering instead.

"Nothing in particular. Lines and circles. It's apparently soothing for the mind to do this. You know, my husband's a lot more skilled at drawing than I am." She held up the napkin. "I call it *Improvisation 1*."

"I was never artistic, myself," he said. "Hated arts and crafts. You know what Wilde said."

"About art being useless?"

"Yes."

A pause. "So...," she said, while putting the crayons away and folding the napkin up and sticking it in her purse. "What are we to do now?"

"What now, what now, what now..." he repeated, thinking.

"Because I can't think of anything."

"I think you wasted your energy on the napkin."

She smiled.

"Do you want to get piss drunk?" he asked.

"Why, do you want to?"

"I'm driving, so...."

She rubbed her nose. "You know what we used to do when I was in high school?" Heath shook his head. "We would just ... drive around in my girlfriend's Datsun - Christ that thing was cramped - and we'd just, drive around on country roads. We'd go so far out, real far, into, near empty fields, wheat fields, and we'd all have the windows down. You had to actually *push* them down because the crank didn't work. And we'd enjoy it. It was somewhat sensual. And we'd have the music on softly - it was a cassette player. It wasn't a constant thing, we didn't, like, do this all the time. But it was so pleasant when we did. We just got away from everything, went to someplace no one else did, and occupied space."

"Sounds like a commercial. A car commercial. You know, peddling freedom and peace and nature. Cars driving through forests, on dirt tracks. No other cars anywhere."

She laughed delicately and nodded her head in approval. "It *does* sound like a commercial, doesn't it? But I swear it was true. We'd chip in for gas and go nowhere."

"You didn't happen to be high or anything when you or all of you did this?"

"No. It was in Massachusetts, where I was born. You know something, when I went on a cross-country trip years ago with friends, through Montana, it was the same exact thing. But we drove through during the day, and I could see the - they call it, 'Big Sky Country.'"

He held out both his hands with his palms facing forward. "*Nothing is more mystical than the plain sky.*"

"What's that?" she asked.

"That would be your slogan! You could sell that."

"Come on! Romanticism, Heath. It is very romantic. Being in nature, driving through nature. That's why the ads sell cars, because they sell that concept, and people like that concept."

He grinned devilishly. "Who did you say you did this with? Old time friends?"

"Well, it started ... well, I can't remember when it started. I do remember we couldn't afford flying, and I've always had this fear of planes."

"I'm not real fond of planes, either, but I think I inherited it from my parents. My biggest problem is motion sickness. Dramamine works, but it makes me so damn tired."

"What really bothered me was how she actually got rid of that car after she got married. I was pissed, I mean, the car still worked. Her parents bought her a Lexus. That Datsun had history."

"Their names?"

"Our little group was Crystal, Janet and myself. The car belonged to Alissa."

"Have you seen any of them since then?"

She waited a moment before responding. "No. We lost touch. Most people lose touch."

Those were the last words uttered until after they paid for the meal and left the restaurant.

sixteen.

Reconstruction

The day had started off incorrectly as the transcript by Stefan read:

8:15: Woke up to alarm clock buzzing.

... and Lucien awoke at 10:15 to an alarm clock playing the radio. Inside, he was irritated by this mistake on his part, but he decided to see if he could make up for lost time - he considered it a challenge. He cautiously got out of bed (so as not to wake Isabella, enjoying her Saturday morning sleep-in) and switched off the radio with expert quickness.

8:30: Showered, shaved and dressed.

After toweling off his face and chest, he put on the white long-sleeved shirt he had laid out for the day and a pair of Dockers khakis.

9:45: My wife [Gina] woke up, got in the shower after me. I took my medication then drove to a pastry shop to buy breakfast. For myself, I had a croissant and a blueberry muffin and for Gina, she got two chocolate éclairs. We both had decaffeinated coffee.

After swallowing a handful of random pills from the one orange container on the counter (he knew which one), he grabbed the keys to Isabella's car and burst out the door yelling, "I'm borrowing your car," though she did not hear him.

———

He returned in pretty good time with the bag of pastries and was balancing the stacked coffee with his chin. When he re-entered his room, Isabella was already out of the shower, combing her wet hair in the bathroom mirror.

"I brought breakfast," Lucien said, setting the coffees down carefully and waving the bag in the air.

"Super," she said, "and you used my car, I'm guessing."

"I bought you two chocolate éclairs."

"Mmm... I don't really like chocolate that much."

He started eating his croissant. "Chocolate is supposed to put you in good spirits, did you know that?"

"My spirits are fine, thank you."

"Your spirits will enjoy the éclairs," he said, and forced her to take the bag.

"I have a neat day planned for us," Lucien said, looking out the window. "You up for some rafting? It's nice out."

seventeen.

While pulling out of the parking lot, Lucien quickly stopped the car.

"What?" Isabella asked. "Did you forget something?"

"Do you know any hardware stores around here?"

"Why?"

"I need to pick up some things before I head back tomorrow and I want to get them before I forget. We have time. Mind?"

"Not at all."

Both traveled to Max's Hardware Store, as per Isabella's instructions. Inside, Lucien found and paid for:

    1 cage for an extremely large dog
    1 100' coil of rope
    1 hacksaw

"Do you have a big pet or something?" she inquired. "Yard work?"

"Actually, no, but we're dog sitting Uga, my cousin's bulldog and Erika - my wife - doesn't like pets. Since I volunteered, I promised to bring back the largest, safest cage I could."

"You're not going to get the cage into the back seat."

"Absolutely not. That's why I'm buying the rope."

"Ohhh," she said, "but won't that scratch the roof of the car?"

"It will be very sturdy."

From the transcript:

> 11:15: After picking up items at the hardware
> store, had our neighbor [name never supplied]
> drive us to the raft site.

Lucien properly tied up the cage and drove it back to the hotel room, dropped off the freshly brought items inside, and then the two of them started walking toward the hotel's front desk.

"Are you hungry?" Lucien asked.

"No."

"Neither am I."

"Do you have to go pee?"

"Excuse me?"

"The bathroom? Do you have to go?"

"No."

The hotel clerk was busy constructing a 1,200 piece jigsaw puzzle of Peter North and Tori Welles fucking when the New Couple entered and stood in front of him.

"Yes?" the clerk blurted out, sounding more like a sigh than a question.

"I need you to do me a big favor again. I'm sorry, I know I'm a pain, but I'll pay you well," Lucien said.

The clerk waited and thought. "Whatever," he said. "Let me get my coat."

———

Lucien instructed the clerk to drive to the site where the homemade raft was parked. The clerk found the whole thing to be unsettling - driving to this place with these people - but understood that it was the moment things were leading to; it was the chance that was going to be taken. Fortunately, he did not need the directions again.

Once there, all three got out and walked toward the raft site, Lucien leading the way, then Isabella following (silent, not asking what's going on) and last, the clerk, a few steps behind her.

Lucien asked the clerk for help pushing the raft - which was (obviously) still where it was left - into the water. Isabella just looked on, frozen, tentative. "I'm not wearing my bathing suit ... and that looks unsafe," she said.

Lucien stopped pushing to comfort/console. "I'm not wearing a suit either. Tell you what - if we wind up in the water, I'll buy you new clothes. Any brand, any style."

"And what if we drown?"

"I went through SCUBA training. I'm a Rescue Diver. I was a lifeguard at Cape May for a summer. You'll be fine."

"It is still not a great idea, at least not now."

"It's a fabulous idea, especially now. It's so succulent and beautiful, shimmering and dirty." Lucien laughed. "It's fun and unexpected. Let's go."

For the first time, Isabella was visibly frightened and started to back away. "I really...," she started, but Lucien grabbed her forcibly by the arm and checked the time on his watch.

11:45: Boarded the raft.

"We are running a little late, dear. We don't have time." He noticed the clerk had made his way up the embankment and back to the car to get away. "Thank you! Pay you later!" he yelled. Back to Isabella: "We don't have time to dawdle. Please? Look - he drove away. We have to. Trust me."

"We're going to end up in the water. That thing is a piece of junk."

"It only looks that way. Stefan used it before - it's fine." A pause. "Come on you beluga whale." He smiled and she couldn't help but lighten up a little. "For me. Please."

She relented, and the two slowly and steadily stepped on the boat, first Lucien, then Isabella (it was designed for and could fit two and only two people on it). Grabbing the long-ish stick from the ground placed conveniently nearby (Lucien got to wondering if Stefan used it - most likely, he figured), he pushed off, casting the raft into the water. They were underway.

"Like in Venice, huh?" he said, looking at her.

"As close as I'll get."

"Why is that?"

"I never had a desire to go."

He nodded. "You know, I still couldn't figure out why he didn't just buy a raft or a canoe or a two-person kayak. They had money."

"You realize how macabre this all seems, right?"

Lucien ignored her.

"Ever go kayaking before?" he asked.

"No."

"River rafting?"

"No."

"Sailing?"

"No."

"Have you ever gone swimming before?"

She gave him a very sarcastic look. "I like the beach but don't like the water."

"I went to a lot of beaches with my family when I was younger. We also went river rafting. The Snake River was pretty neat."

Isabella wrapped her arms around her chest.

"Cold?"

"A little."

"You never exactly explained why you went with Stefan in the first place. Attraction? Wealth?"

"I don't know." She thought for a bit. "He seemed ... and it sounds funny ... but he seemed, just ... nice. You know? Someone friendly. Reserved and quiet but really eager to, to ... he really liked to talk and share stories and I found him interesting. He wasn't out to ruin anybody's day."

"Pity?"

"Did I say pity? Well, to some extent."

"And boredom."

"Well ... no, I wouldn't say boredom."

"There are lots of other guys around. Grab one of them."

"I'm not sure a lot of them are what I'm looking for," she said.

Lucien scoffed. "And he was? Maybe it was the allure of being with a married man."

"There must be a million married men out there, trust me. Most men are married. You included." She smiled.

He smiled too, but turned away.

"I hope I'm not asking too many questions," he said.

"I understand you are just making conversation. I know you told me you have a job to do."

Lucien ran through his mental list of questions to figure out where to lead her next. "Did he--?"

But she interrupted. "You know what he loved? Board games. We'd sit on my living room floor and play *Connect Four*, drink some Peach Schnapps and maybe put on a movie in the background. Something we've seen before but admire the parts of - we'd ignore most of the picture except for the parts we liked and then stopped playing to watch. The movies were almost always comedies."

"I'm privy to backgammon, myself," Lucien volunteered.

"We didn't play that. Chess. On occasion. Other times we played *Mouse Trap*, *Hungry, Hungry Hippos* and *Operation*. Kid games. Fun, silly stuff. I never minded. It was always a blast and better than just bar-hopping."

"Did you like his wife?"

"She was all right, I suppose. I honestly never carried on a genuine conversation with her. She loved remodeling the house, doing watercolors with those step-by-step books you can never emulate, tanning. Her skin was the color of French toast. She liked Panama-type hats...."

Lucien laughed. "French toast?"

"Golden brown. You've seen pictures. Her skin looked all the more dark because of her large white hats, plain white dress shirts. Open. Flowing. Like she was a poster girl for some Caribbean Island. Stefan never complained about her or mentioned her. He was very reserved like that."

"Did he ever hit you?" he asked.

Isabella was taken aback. "Never. I wouldn't put up with that."

"Never?"

"Never."

"Did you ever hit him?"

"I'm not the hitting kind."

"Am I?" Lucien inquired.

"You?"

"Certainly." He waited for the worst.

"All men are of the hitting kind."

She waited a moment for him to respond.

"I don't agree with you, but it's interesting," he remarked.

eighteen.

"Here looks like the spot where we should park this," Lucien said, aiming toward the shore at the end of their journey. "I remember the gaudy maroon-colored house on the hill over there." He pointed down river.

She fixed her hair, adjusted her clothing. "Even if we're far away I don't mind walking."

1:30: Docked boat, walked back to house.

Lucien stepped off first and his shoes landed just to the right of a soft patch of mud. "Be careful where you step," he warned as he took Isabella's hand and guided her to safety. "Fun, huh?"

"It was different."

"Do you have a key to his house?" he asked, wanting to take a free tour.

"I did ... but flushed it."

"Paranoia."

She nodded. "Got rid of everything."

"Even *Connect Four*?"

"The games are probably still in his house."

———

They walked about forty-five minutes back to the hotel - it turned out Lucien was thinking of another gaudy maroon house on a hill. Isabella was complaining of being chilled and having a sinus headache, so back in the room Lucien gave her two Advil and a glass of water laced with a potent multitude of sleeping drugs taken from a few choice bottles and with a 'recipe' he found out about in another case of his from a while back.

"Here," he said, "take these and wash it all down with this. Works like a charm."

> 2:00: Drugged Gina with prepared syringe...
> (Not having any syringes or things like that available to him - Lucien had a fear of needles - he deviated in his method of 'drugging' from the template.)

"Would you like to go out later? Maybe a nearby town?"

"That would be fine. I just need a little time to rest before we do."

In less than an hour, Isabella would find herself fluctuating between unconsciousness and consciousness, eyelids heavy and unable to move.

nineteen.

Lucien was sitting, cross-legged, directly across from the giant dog cage he had purchased earlier in the day, with Isabella stripped naked and twisted up inside. She was still breathing, and this fascinated him. He was staring at the top of her chest, moving up and down so delicately.

In good time he got up and brought over a stack of white printer paper and some India ink. He folded up one sheet in half and spread the ink all over the one-side and folded the paper. When he opened it, it was still wet and he blew on it to dry it. He did that with nine more papers, making ten in all.

He ventured back over to the cage, and again sat directly across. The image of a woman, contorted into an inhuman shape and motionless was at once repelling and alluring. He raised one of his papers in the air.

"Technically, these are unscientific because there is no real definitive way to test what they mean or what the subject's responses mean, unlike, well, a multiple-choice battery on depression, like, for example, the Beck Depression Inventory. But they *are* neat to look at. Tell me, what do you think of this? Hmm?" He tapped on the cage. "How does it make you feel? Does it look like an animal? A zebra? A zebra. Ze-*bras* maybe."

He rolled up the paper into a tube and pushed it halfway into the cage. He raised the next one.

"Flowers, right. Insects. So uninvolving."

He stuffed the rest of the papers into the cage.

"You okay?" he asked.

3:00: Looted house, threw Gina's belongings into
the trash.

Lucien walked over to the bed and picked up her purse.
He opened it and began taking some of the objects out.

"Oh, guys need stuff like this, believe it or not. Pockets
don't work. That's why single guys' cars look like hell
inside. The car is a purse with wheels."

He took the two tubes of lipstick that were in the purse
and threw them at the cage. He took out her wallet and
change purse and stuffed the $10.20 she had left and put it
in his pocket. The breath spray, compact mirror, tampons,
tissues, sugarless chewing gum, credit cards and a little toy
bear the size of a human thumb were also shoved inside the
cage.

3:30: Cleaned up the rest of the room.

———

On the living room floor, Harold, who Erika preferred
over Heath (but it was basically a toss-up), was lying
naked, except for a pair of gray boxers, surrounded by and
covered with hot pancakes and maple syrup. Erika was
standing on top of him, in her bra and panties (the former
undone and ready to slide off) pouring Aunt Jemima syrup
all over his face and chest. The more he laughed the more
she poured, the more she poured the more frantic he
became, causing her to step down even harder on his greasy
flesh.

"You can't deny it smells great," Harold said, trying to
grab Erika's ankles and trip her onto the sticky, spongy
floor.

"I also like the smell of gasoline," she said, and both of them kept laughing.

"So do I!" he agreed.

She wedged her right foot in his right armpit and her left foot in his left armpit. "It's like I'm standing on wet fish," she said.

He nodded and smiled, and was sucking on a section of pancake that had fallen out of Erika's hair and landed next to his right ear.

twenty.

In a short while, the hotel room was tidied up and taken care of: the cage was mysteriously missing, the countertops cleaned off, the papers disposed of, the drawings (previously adorning the one wall) were put away. Lucien had to do a quick but efficient clean-up job because he had extensive documenting left to do: typing, proofreading, and printing out all pertinent and relevant details. Upon completion and many hours of work, he constructed a 90-page document, as accurate and precise as he could make with the resources he had. Around 11:30, while the document was printing, he ran to the local 24-hr. 7-Eleven to buy two Hostess Apple Pies and a bottle of Fiji water. He fell asleep after 12:20.

———

The next morning, he checked out of the hotel, and once more coerced the hotel clerk to drive him to the shop where his car was being 'repaired' (he tipped the clerk $100 for all his efforts, for which the clerk was more than pleased). He paid for his car repairs with cash and left without uttering a single work except "Thanks." The mechanic, on the other hand, was full of questions and statements and jabbered away about things Lucien had no time to deal with and nodded and walked away.

Upon receiving the car, he drove it back to the hotel once more, loaded up his belongings (being kept in the hotel's main office), and started on his journey back home.

twenty-one.

Lucien drove his BMW slowly down the street, not just zooming around the way he normally did, because he noticed, a while back, that there was a car parked in the driveway that was neither his nor his wife's nor anyone's he knew of - a red Toyota Celica. He parked his car on the opposite side of the street and approached the house.

While walking up, he spotted on the sidewalk the teacup that he had left there before he departed on his trip. It was still sitting there, in the exact same spot, but instead of 1/4 cup of tea, it was completely filled with rainwater and a single leaf. He approached the foreign car and peeked inside, but the car was empty.

Along the side of the house were the garbage cans filled with crushed bags and boxes from the International House of Pancakes.

He tiptoed around the house and tried to look inside the windows, but they were covered with newspaper. He checked his watch, and decided to get back inside his own car and find a proper place to spend the night.

———

Lucien pulled up to Jacob's house, Jacob who was still single, Jacob who owed him a few favors. He could have stayed in another hotel, but that didn't sound too promising to him. He knew who he could depend on.

He rang the doorbell. Jacob opened it.

"I'm so glad you're home," Lucien said.

"What's up?"

"I need your help. Can I come in?"

Jacob stepped out of the way so Lucien could enter. "Sit where you like."

———

Lucien told Jacob what happened, or at least a variation of the truth - his idea of the truth - and was hoping Jacob would be mildly sympathetic.

"I still don't believe this," Jacob said, staring right into Lucien, the two of them seated comfortably in the living room, under a multitude of framed pictures covering the walls - all of them done with crayon on 8 x 8 pieces of cloth.

"Can I stay here for just a bit? Two, three days?"

"Why didn't you just stay single? Why did you have to get married?"

Lucien shrugged. "We're designed for each other. Lids for pots, as they say."

"Don't be ridiculous."

Lucien got up and started walking to the front door. "I'm going to get my things, if that's okay with you."

Jacob sighed. "No problem at all. You can sleep on the big couch."

twenty-two

Jacob and Lucien decided to take their coffee in the den, a room completely devoid of chairs, windows or decorations aside from a stone pillar sitting in the middle of the room with a little dollhouse resting on top of it, plastic and ivory, and open on the one side so you could look in and rearrange the people and furniture. Jacob kept it from a previous relationship and never talked about it. All he ever said about it was how he considered the dollhouse a good luck charm.

Since the room didn't have chairs, the two men had brought into the den several pillows and their cups. They were seated on the floor.

"So you saw some stranger's car parked out front...," Jacob repeated.

"It was 9:30 in the morning. Think: who would be there at 9:30 in the morning?"

"Did you look inside? Maybe it was a salesman or a plumber and you're overreacting. Maybe it's a friend of hers."

"No. It wasn't any of those."

"You didn't have to go on this trip you just decided to go on. You know it wasn't necessary."

"Necessity wasn't the point."

Jacob rubbed his eyes. "Well, whatever. That's finished. I keep thinking you're just playing out the worst-case scenario."

There was a long pause where the two just sat and had nothing to do but enjoy their hot drinks.

"Now what?" Jacob asked.

"We could...."

"What?"

"I'm curious if they're there now."

Jacob sighed. "Oh, come on."

"I want to go."

"The car is probably gone."

"I have to know."

Pause.

"Fine. I'll drive," Jacob said.

———

Jacob's car rolled down the street slowly, the same way Lucien had earlier on in the day (the neighborhood was typically quiet). The mysterious automobile was still in the driveway.

"Is that it?" Jacob asked.

"I'll be damned."

"We need to go inside."

"And be humiliated?"

"I want to try the window again," Lucien said, and opened his door.

"Stay here."

"I feel like slashing tires."

"Don't be stupid."

"I always knew. Always. Couldn't prove it, though."

"It's embarrassing, I realize."

"It's about trust." Lucien walked around the car. Jacob got out, grabbed him, and forced him to get back in. "We're leaving. Deal with it when you've cooled down. You don't need her. Let's go."

Lucien relented, and the two returned to Jacob's home.

twenty-three.

The Court Room was half-full, but most of those in attendance were familiar faces that Lucien remembered from Montgomery, people he had seen in bars, the lady with the garden, Mr. Lacroix and his secretary, Erika by herself. Only Isabella was missing. A lot was said and a lot was asked, the jury sat and listened attentively, preparing to pass judgment because they were asked to. Lucien sat with Stefan, in front of them a large stack of papers. Lucien felt no urge to say more than he did, and did not confer with Stefan at all, nor did Stefan confer with him.

The amount of time passed was great, and the exact duration of the trial itself would be a matter of opinion. As it endured, the people never flagged in their interest, always drawn in. Stefan sat motionless and stared at his lap.

The only words the two engaged in came after the judge and jury issued the appropriate punishment. Erika had begun crying. Stefan looked at her, and then turned to Lucien: "Where was Isabella? Did you find her?"

"She couldn't come," Lucien answered, "but she wished you good luck."

And never another word was uttered between the two of them again.

———

In the hallway, Erika had waited for Lucien to exit and then, when she spotted him, she did not hesitate to approach him and follow him out. He was carrying his stack of papers.

"Where were you all this time?" she inquired, not enraged but mostly curious.

"Didn't you get my voice mail? I'm going home now."

The two left in separate cars and arrived at home within five minutes of each other.

Lucien took all of the objects out of his car and brought them inside to be cleaned or put away. He threw his laundry in the hamper, set his laptop and printer back on the desk, stored his toiletries back in the bathroom, lined up the prescription bottles on the counter and put the stack of transcripts and notes on the kitchen table for filing. (When seeing them, Erika said dismissively, "Little good those did," making sure Lucien could hear.)

He also made sure to bring in the teacup he left outside, dumped the rainwater onto the grass and placed it in the sink to be washed with detergent.

twenty-four.

It was night-time, Lucien had cut the power to the house, and Erika was on the kitchen floor, breathing but doped up and temporarily unconscious. Above her, on the kitchen table: four orange pill containers.

Utilizing this time wisely - the dosage she unknowingly took was not *that* strong - Lucien got out several candles and matches and used them as his light. With thumbtacks, he covered the walls of the upstairs and downstairs of the house with transcripts from the case and his drawings. (When he realized that he was running low on things to tack up, he went through his Archives, posting old cases and transcripts as well.) Volumes of words and distorted sketches covered the windows, ceiling, refrigerator, the doors plus the television set. After completing this great task and being exhausted, he collapsed in a chair, the candle still lit in his hand.

———

Erika woke up earlier than she probably should have, given the dosage and her weight - medications don't always last as long as they should, sadly - and was frightened to find herself in the same clothes as the previous day, and laying on the kitchen floor. She examined the papers on the walls, and then saw her husband fast asleep in a chair. She rushed over to the phone to call for help, but the line was cut. The upstairs telephone line was cut as well. Soon after, she found the cell phone and her car keys and ran out of the house.

———

In twenty minutes she returned, not with the police, but with Heath (who brought his own car), who she had confidence in and trusted to lend assistance. Heath showed clear signs of disgust with the new house decorations.

"Exactly what the hell is going on? What is all this?" He ripped one of the papers off the wall and read it. "Did you put this up?" He was directing his question to the dreaming Lucien, still in the chair.

Heath repeated his question, but louder, and Lucien still did not stir. He grabbed him by the shirt collar and shook him. This woke him up and he began to groan.

Lucien opened his eyes. "Who are you? What are you doing here?"

"Why did you do this?" Heath shouted.

"I don't know."

Heath grabbed fistfuls of shirt and lifted up a limp Lucien. "That's it. We're going."

Lucien came to and fought against him - the two tussled and pushed and shoved. Heath, out of nowhere, clocked him with a right hook, and Lucien staggered. He followed that with several more punches, all making direct contact to the face, and Lucien was unconscious once more.

Each of them grabbed a leg and dragged the deadweight outside and into Erika's car.

"What do you want me to do now?" Heath asked.

"Just toss him someplace."

"What's that going to solve? He'll come to and be back."

"I don't care," was all she could say.

Heath and Erika drove about fifteen minutes along a barren stretch of road and pushed him out of the car head first, making sure to scrape some of his scalp on the asphalt. They then turned around and sped back home, guilt-free.

twenty-five.

In due time, Lucien regained consciousness, wiped the blood off his face, stood up and cautiously staggered down the road, dizzy and in obvious pain. He was still wearing his pajamas, and covered in dirt, but grateful the road he was left on received a minimal amount of traffic, for he would have surely been run over otherwise.

He found a run-down gas station miles down the road - he was lucky it was not farther, because his focus and stability were completely off. He went inside the office and spoke to the mechanic behind the counter, who took pity on him but secretly wondered if he should call the police. Not wanting to spoil his day, he simply let Lucien use the office phone, with which he dialed Jacob's cell phone number.

Lucien waited outside until Jacob showed up, and while sitting on the curb became concerned that his directions were inaccurate. They were not, however, and in due time Jacob arrived.

"Oh Jesus," was all he said, seeing his ragged friend in his nightwear.

Lucien got in the car. "Do you have any weapons?"

"Come on, now."

"I am not joking."

"Calm down. I'm getting tired of being in this ... sick charade. I am taking you to the hospital."

"No you are not. I need to relax. Take me to your house."

———

In his den, Jacob was wearing brand-new yellow cleaning gloves for wiping down the shotgun he kept in a cabinet with Fantastik all-purpose cleaner. Lucien, having showered, applied Neosporin antibiotic cream to his forehead (and several Band-aids), swallowed some Demerol and put on Jacob's clothes (a white long-sleeve shirt and black dress pants). He was standing in the doorway and laughed at Jacob for bothering to clean the gun.

"I wouldn't do this for just anyone," his friend said.

Lucien smiled. "At this rate I feel like I'm indebted to you for life. I appreciate it and I want you to know that."

Jacob inspected the barrels by pointing the gun at the ceiling light. "This thing's not mine, you realize."

"Whose is it?"

"It was my father's. Mom mailed it to me for safekeeping."

A pause.

"Where are the shells?" Lucien asked.

twenty-six.

Outside of Lucien's house, the foreign car still sat - it belonged, he now knew, to the man Erika brought over earlier in the day and kicked him out of his own house. Both Lucien and Jacob played Detective for hours, sitting outside, in Jacob's car, doing surveillance, waiting with undeniable patience. They spent the entire night outside. Coffee and Mountain Dew and Vivarin and Sudafed kept them alert.

It wouldn't be until 8 AM the next morning that Heath would emerge from the house, get in his Celica, and leave the area. Jacob and Lucien, wide-eyed and ready, started the car and followed him. The shotgun was in the back seat.

As it turned out, Heath lived on the bottom floor of a two-floor apartment building on the other side of town. Jacob, Lucien's personal chauffeur, parked about two blocks away from the building as per Lucien's request (Jacob thought this was too far, but Lucien, not thinking, insisted). Heath got out of his car and entered the front door. Lucien emerged from the car he was in, and carried the loaded shotgun with him - in plain-view - to the front door.

Heath had not been inside for three minutes and had to answer the knock on the door. The instant he unlocked it and pulled the door open, Lucien forced his way in, SWAT-style, with the shotgun aimed right at Heath's head. Lucien kicked the door shut with his right leg.

"Now I'm in your house," Lucien said.

Heath was backing up and trembling. "Whoa, whoa," he said as he was trying to move his face outside the barrel's range.

"I want you to get on your knees," Lucien demanded, pressing the end of the barrel against Heath's closed lips and down at an angle, forcing him to sink to the floor. "Open," he said, and pushed the gun into skin with even more pressure.

Heath kept mumbling "Please" and "No" through clenched teeth but it did little good. The blast was so loud - and Lucien so unaccustomed to it - that he, himself, was startled by the bang and the tinnitus-esque ringing in his ears. On the floor was the remains of a face, on the coffee table a framed picture of Heath and another man giving the 'thumbs up' at some tropical resort, the bookshelf devoid of books but filled with an assortment of empty liquor bottles.

Lucien thought about dropping the shotgun and just running, but he decided, instead to take it with him. He started for the door.

Upstairs, getting dressed to begin his own day was Harold, who, apparently, was Heath's brother. The two rarely spoke to each other or meddled in each other's business, and had a poor relationship altogether. It was Harold, upstairs, that heard the blast, and it was Harold, the quick thinker, who looked outside to see Lucien half-running down the street with gun in hand. Not understanding what happened, but reacting out of instinct, he yelled to Lucien to stop, a scream that Lucien could not hear with his head buzzing. Reacting with precision timing, he grabbed the baseball bat from the closet - it was the only think he thought of as a weapon (in that instant) and gave chase, flying down the stairs and outside.

Being of youthful disposition - more youthful than Lucien, at least, by a few years and in overall better shape - Harold took him in the race down the street. Before Lucien could turn around with the shotgun, Harold swung the bat, connecting with the back of Lucien's skull. When Lucien hit the ground, face first, he was twitching, and with all the adrenaline running through Harold, he reacted to the twitching with another swing - this time he connected with the side of the head. When he looked up, he saw that the vehicle Lucien was running towards was no longer there.

twenty-seven.

The clock alarm buzzed at 6:40, which was when Harold always got up no matter what time he went to bed (he was a light sleeper and always had been). Erika was not used to this, and the alarm clock acted as an unending nuisance to her.

Harold jumped up, put on his slippers, turned off the alarm and headed straight for the bathroom.

Erika, groggy, said, "I'll never get used to this."

"My lower back hurts like hell," he said while standing in front of the sink, rummaging through the medicine cabinet.

"Take some Advil," she advised.

"I am."

He showered and shaved most quickly, and got dressed and ran out the door without eating or saying goodbye.

Erika forced herself up at 7:45, and it was a burden having to walk to the bathroom. She decided to take some Advil too, because she had a throbbing headache. But she never did get to open the medicine cabinet, or shower, or put on deodorant, for what happened before all that prevented her from doing so, for the floor was wet and she slipped, and the sink's cold surface met flesh, and darkness came into the picture because of the simple slip and from that developed something like shock. Paralysis, unconsciousness ... the events that followed (too late to help, alas) could never be known by the victim: anxiety, panic, bright lights. It's true: accidents arise and threaten, a voice, somewhere, said. Another merely sounded concerned that it could happen to her. Suddenly, everyone walked away. People look upon such things with pity, for they know it could happen to them, or to their loved ones. And on the table was another collection of still organs and flesh and matter. It was like what happened to the great William Holden. It was so ethereal and white and instant. It was also the month of July.

———

Sitting in Lucien's chair, in Lucien's office, Harold was indulging in his breakfast: a pre-made container of mixed-fruit and a large cup of coffee, black. The office was cluttered with papers, files, all out of order, all next to each other. Bills couldn't possibly be found.

Jacob knocked lightly on the door, and then peeked in.

"Good morning!" Harold said.

"What time did you get here? Lots of work, I can see."

"Since I have to go to the Court House I need to take care of all this ... back flow."

"What you need is another secretary."

Harold scoffed. "Can't get the one I got to show up."

A pause. "Wait - which one is it today? Don't tell me it's Delphine Whitney."

He nodded and sighed. "She hasn't got a prayer."

———

The drive to the Court House was a familiar one, not anything to look forward to. You passed the same things, the same houses, the same trees. It wasn't like driving through a bustling downtown somewhere, where the sights of people you might know could be passing by and enjoying breakfast on the go.

The bridge that Harold drove over was still there, and so was the river that flowed beneath it, low from lack of rain. Down river, some 300 feet, along the edge, if you were hiking or fishing, or wandering around, you might notice a man-made raft with a cage tied to it, stuck along the side, caught up in the rocks and tree limbs long separated from their previous owners. Inside the cage, even if you looked close enough, you couldn't tell what you were seeing, but you would, unquestionably, know that it was silent.

www.ingramcontent.com/pod-product-compliance
Lightning Source LLC
Chambersburg PA
CBHW020548130626
46552CB00007B/2814